The Signal-Man

A Classic Ghost Story of Fate, Premonition, and Tragedy on the Rails

A Modern Translation

Adapted for the Contemporary Reader

Charles Dickens

Translated by Tim Zengerink

Table of Contents

Preface - Message to the Reader 1

Introduction 4

The Signal Man 9

Thank You for Reading 25

Preface - Message to the Reader

What If You Could Help Rebuild the Greatest Library in Human History?

Thousands of years ago, the Library of Alexandria stood as the crown jewel of human achievement — a sanctuary where the collected wisdom of every known civilization was gathered, preserved, and shared freely.

And then, it was lost.

Through fire, conquest, and the slow erosion of time, humanity lost not just books — but ideas, dreams, discoveries, and stories that could have changed the world forever.

Today, the Library of Alexandria lives again — and you are invited to be a part of its restoration.

Our mission is simple yet profound:

To rebuild the greatest library the world has ever known, and to translate all timeless works into every language and dialect, so that no seeker of knowledge is ever left behind again.

By joining our movement to rebuild the modern Library of Alexandria, you become part of an unprecedented mission:

- **Unlimited Access to the Greatest Audiobooks & eBooks Ever Written:**

  Instantly explore thousands of legendary works—Plato, Shakespeare, Jane Austen, Leo Tolstoy, and countless more. All instantly available to read or listen, placing a complete literary universe at your fingertips.

- **Beautiful Paperback & Deluxe Editions at Printing Cost**

  Own any title as an elegant paperback, deluxe hardcover, or stunning collectible boxset—offered to you at true printing cost, delivered straight to your door. Build your personal Library of Alexandria, crafted for beauty, built for durability, and worthy of proud display.

- **Fresh Translations for Modern Readers—in Every Language & Dialect**

  Enjoy timeless masterpieces reimagined in clear, contemporary language—no more outdated phrases or obscure references. Alongside the original versions, we're tirelessly translating these classics into every language and dialect imaginable, ensuring accessibility and understanding across cultures and generations.

- **Join a Global Renaissance of Literature & Knowledge**

  You directly support expanding our library, publishing deluxe editions at true cost, translating works into all global languages, and bringing humanity's greatest stories to people everywhere. By joining today, you're not just preserving a legacy of masterpieces; you set in motion a powerful wave of literary accessibility.

Become a Torchbearer of Knowledge.

Join us for free now at **LibraryofAlexandria.com**

Together, we will ensure that the light of human wisdom never fades again.

With gratitude and a shared love of knowledge,

The Modern Library of Alexandria Team

Visit:

www.libraryofalexandria.com

Or scan the code below:

Introduction

Ghosts, Guilt,
and the Limits of Human Understanding

Charles Dickens's The Signal-Man, first published in 1866 in All the Year Round, stands as one of the most haunting, psychologically layered, and elegantly constructed ghost stories in the English literary tradition. Though it is brief in length—just a few thousand words—it contains a depth of emotion, ambiguity, and philosophical inquiry that rivals full-length novels. The story is frequently included in anthologies of Victorian ghost tales, and with good reason. It is not only a chilling narrative of supernatural terror, but a meditation on fate, foreknowledge, isolation, and the tragic impossibility of preventing disaster.

At the heart of the tale is a simple yet terrifying premise: a railway signalman is haunted by ghostly visions that appear just before fatal accidents occur. He is a man marked by duty, vigilance, and loneliness, tormented by warnings he cannot fully interpret and powerless to act upon them. The story's narrator—a curious outsider—visits the signalman's lonely post and listens to his strange tale, only to discover, in the final twist, that the man's doom was itself foreshadowed by the same spectral signs he had so desperately tried to decipher.

What makes The Signal-Man endure is not only its mastery of atmosphere or its haunting twist ending, but the profound sense of dread it evokes—not from ghosts, but from the realization that understanding the future does not empower us to change it. Dickens, writing just a few years after the traumatic Staplehurst rail accident in which he was personally involved and nearly killed, imbues this story with a deep awareness of trauma, helplessness, and the ways in which modern technology—specifically the railway—brings not only speed and progress, but death and dehumanization.

This introduction will explore the rich thematic and structural complexities of The Signal-Man, its place within Dickens's broader body of work, and its unique contribution to the development of supernatural fiction. We will examine its psychological resonance, its symbolic use of space and machinery, and the ways in which it anticipates modern anxieties about communication, precognition, and the mechanization of human life. Though small in scope, The Signal-Man offers a vast and disturbing insight into the human condition—and the ghosts that dwell not only beyond the grave, but in the mind, the future, and the fatal silence between warning and tragedy.

Modernity, Isolation, and the Machinery of Doom

From the first paragraph, Dickens constructs a world defined by shadow, echo, and disconnection. The story opens with the narrator calling down into a railway cutting, where the signalman stands at the bottom of a steep embankment, surrounded by stone walls, a dark tunnel, and a single red light. The setting is almost mythic in its symbolism—an underworld of sorts, removed from natural light and sound, where the signalman lives like a sentinel between life and death. He is not merely a railway worker. He is a guardian at the edge of the unknown.

This setting is not incidental. By the 1860s, the railway was the symbol of modernity in Victorian Britain—a marvel of engineering that had revolutionized travel, commerce, and communication. But it was also a source of immense danger and anxiety. Train crashes were horrifyingly common, and the machinery of the railway was cold, indifferent, and relentless. In The Signal-Man, Dickens captures this duality: the marvel and the menace. The signalman's job is to control the flow of this great system, yet he is rendered helpless in the face of the very accidents he is meant to prevent.

The signalman himself is an extraordinary character. He is educated, articulate, and thoughtful—qualities that contrast sharply with his lowly position and intense loneliness. He takes his duty seriously, almost religiously, and this makes his psychological torment all the more poignant. The appearance of the ghost—a figure that warns of impending doom but never explains it—shatters his sense of order and usefulness. He is given knowledge, but no power. He sees the signs, but cannot interpret them in time to prevent tragedy.

This theme—of foreknowledge without agency—is central to the story's horror. The signalman is not insane. He is lucid, sincere, and credible. But he is doomed to be ignored, both by the ghost and by the narrator. The specter offers no clarity. The narrator offers no belief. The signalman is caught in a tragic loop of seeing, dreading, and failing—until he becomes, in the final twist, the subject of his own premonition.

In this way, Dickens uses the ghost not as a vehicle of punishment or revenge, but as a symbol of fatal repetition. The signalman does everything right. He performs his duty. He tells his story. He asks for help. But the system—the railway, the machinery, the world—moves forward regardless. The ghost does not speak. The train does not stop. And the man dies exactly as he feared he would.

This is not supernatural justice. It is existential despair.

The Ghost as Symbol: Premonition, Trauma, and the Limits of Reason

In contrast to many Victorian ghost stories that feature haunted houses, vengeful spirits, or religious morality, The Signal-Man presents a haunting rooted in psychological and technological uncertainty. The ghost does not scream, wail, or threaten. It merely stands, silently gesturing—a haunting image repeated three times, each preceding a catastrophe. The signalman interprets these appearances not as delusions, but as messages. But the messages are incomplete. The ghost is not a guide, but an enigma.

This use of the ghost as a symbol of incomplete information reflects the modern anxiety about knowledge without meaning. In a world increasingly dominated by machines, signals, and systems, Dickens suggests that the human being—the individual mind—is often left unable to connect the dots. The signalman receives signals he cannot decode. He hears words without context. He is haunted not by guilt or sin, but by not knowing what he is supposed to know.

This haunting aligns with Dickens's own traumatic experience. In 1865, just a year before writing the story, Dickens survived the Staplehurst rail crash, in which several people were killed and many more injured. He was deeply affected by the event, and scholars have long noted its influence on The Signal-Man. The story's obsession with impending disaster, the fear of mechanical failure, and the helplessness of individuals caught in industrial accidents all reflect the emotional residue of that experience.

But the story goes deeper. It also explores the human mind's fragile relationship with time and destiny. The signalman's visions are prophetic, but they offer no salvation. They arrive too early to be useful, too late to be prevented. This ambiguity creates a moral and existential paralysis. The story suggests that knowing the future is not only useless—it may be psychologically destructive.

This anticipates later literary and philosophical treatments of fate, including Kafka, Camus, and the entire genre of speculative horror. It asks: If we cannot act on foreknowledge, is it better not to know? Is ignorance preferable to powerless awareness? And in a world where technology moves faster than comprehension, are we not all signalmen, staring into the tunnel, waiting for a disaster we cannot name?

Dickens leaves these questions unanswered. He allows the ghost to remain unexplained. He gives us no final moral. Instead, he offers an image: a man alone in a dark cutting, listening for a signal, seeing a figure, raising his hand, and dying—just as the figure did, in warning, days before.

It is this unresolved dread that gives The Signal-Man its lasting power. It is not a ghost story in the conventional sense. It is a tragedy of perception, a parable of helplessness, and a meditation on the impossibility of changing what is to come.

In the silence after the story ends, we do not hear screams.

We hear the whistle of the train. The rush of metal. The echo of a voice that cannot be answered.

And that, Dickens tells us, is the real haunting. Not the ghost itself, but the signal unheard. The warning unheeded. The future, inevitable, just around the bend.

The Signal Man

"Hey! Down there!"

When he heard me call out, he was standing just outside his work post, holding a flag that was wrapped tightly around its pole. You'd think, because of how the land was shaped, he'd know exactly where the voice came from. But instead of looking up toward where I was—standing at the top of the steep slope above him—he turned and looked down the railway. There was something strange about the way he did it, though I couldn't explain what it was. Still, it caught my attention. Even though he stood deep down in the trench, with shadows all around him, I was standing high above in the red glow of a setting sun. I had to shade my eyes just to see him.

"Hey! Down there!" I called again.

He stopped looking down the tracks and slowly turned back around. Then he lifted his eyes and saw me up above him.

"Is there a way for me to come down and talk to you?" I asked.

He didn't answer, just stared up at me. I didn't want to push, so I waited. Suddenly, I felt a strange shaking in the ground and in the air—it quickly grew stronger, and then a loud rush of sound made me step back, like it might pull me over the edge. A train flew by below, sending up a mist that rose to where I stood, then drifted off across the land. When it passed, I looked down and saw him rolling his flag back up.

I asked again if there was a way down. He paused and stared at me for a moment, then pointed with his rolled-up flag to a spot a few hundred feet away on my level. "All right!" I called back, and headed that way. After a bit of looking around, I found a rough zigzag path carved into the side of the slope, and I followed it down.

The path was steep and the walls on either side were damp stone, getting wetter the farther I went. Because of that, it took a while to reach the bottom, and during the walk, I kept thinking about the odd, almost unwilling way he had shown me where to go.

Once I had gone far enough down to see him again, I noticed he was standing right between the tracks where the train had just passed. It looked like he was waiting for me. His left hand was on his chin, and his left elbow rested on his right arm, which was crossed over his chest. He looked like someone deep in thought, watching and waiting. It made me stop and wonder.

I kept walking. When I stepped onto the level ground and got closer, I saw that he was a pale man with a dark beard and thick eyebrows. His job post was one of the loneliest, bleakest places I'd ever seen. On both sides were wet, jagged stone walls that blocked the view of everything except a narrow strip of sky. In one direction, the view stretched into a long, crooked passage that felt like a prison. The other way ended in a dark red light and the mouth of a tunnel that looked cold and unfriendly, with heavy, harsh architecture. Hardly any sunlight ever reached this place—it smelled damp and lifeless. A cold wind swept through it, and I felt like I'd stepped out of the real world into something colder and less human.

I got close enough to touch him, but still he didn't move or stop staring at me. Then he took one step back and raised his hand.

"This is a lonely job," I said. "It caught my attention when I looked down from up there. I guess you don't get many visitors—but I hope they're welcome when they come?"

I told him I was just a regular man who had spent most of his life in small, confined places, and now that I was free to go where I wanted, I was curious about these kinds of places and jobs. I'm not sure exactly how I said it—I've never been great at starting conversations—but something about him made me nervous.

He glanced over at the red light near the tunnel. He studied it carefully, almost like he expected to see something that wasn't there. Then he looked back at me.

"That light—is it part of your job?" I asked.

He spoke quietly. "Don't you know it is?"

A strange thought suddenly hit me. I stared at his fixed eyes and serious face and wondered: was he even real? Could he be a ghost?

Later, I thought maybe his mind wasn't all right, that maybe something had happened to him.

I stepped back, unsure. But as I moved, I saw something in his eyes—a flicker of fear, like he was scared of me. That quickly pushed the strange thought away.

"You're looking at me," I said, trying to smile, "like you're afraid of me."

"I wasn't sure," he said, "if I'd seen you before."

"Where do you mean?" I asked.

He pointed toward the red signal light.

"There?" I asked.

He stared at me closely and nodded silently.

"My friend, why would I be down there? Whatever you think, I've never been to that place—you can be sure of that."

"I believe you," he said. "Yes, I'm sure."

He seemed more at ease now, and so did I. He responded to my questions easily and spoke clearly. I asked if he had a lot of work to do. He said his job came with responsibility, but not much physical labor. He mainly had to be alert and precise. His tasks were to change the signal, adjust the lights, and pull a lever every now and then.

As for the long, lonely hours I had mentioned, he said that was just the way his life had settled. He was used to it now. During that time, he had taught himself to recognize another language—at least well enough to read it and guess how it might sound. He had also tried to study math, like fractions and a bit of algebra, but admitted that even as a child, numbers were never his strength.

Did he always have to stay down in that damp, narrow space during his shift? Couldn't he ever come up into the sunlight? He said it depended. At certain times, there was less traffic on the railway, and depending on the hour and weather, he could sometimes step above the shadows. Still, because he always had to be ready to respond to his electric signal bell—and always listened for it with extra focus—the little breaks he got didn't feel very restful.

He invited me into his small work shelter. Inside, there was a fire, a desk for logging reports, a telegraph machine, and the bell he'd mentioned earlier. I told him—hoping it wouldn't sound rude—that he seemed very well-educated, maybe more than most people in jobs like his. He replied that situations like his weren't rare. You'd find people working in all sorts of jobs where their backgrounds didn't quite match their current roles—in places like workhouses, the police, and even the army. He said the railway was no different.

When he was younger (though, sitting in that little hut, it was hard for either of us to believe), he'd studied science and attended lectures.

But then he lost his way, wasted his chances, and never recovered from it. He didn't complain about it, though. He accepted that he had made his choices and now had to live with them. He said it was far too late to change direction.

He told me all of this in a calm voice, occasionally glancing between me and the fire. Every now and then, he'd politely say "Sir," especially when talking about his past—like he wanted me to understand he wasn't pretending to be anything more than what I saw.

While we talked, the little bell interrupted him a few times. He read incoming messages and sent responses. Once, he had to step outside to wave his flag as a train passed and give the driver a quick message. I noticed how careful and focused he was during these tasks—he would stop mid-sentence and remain silent until everything was done.

Honestly, I would have thought he was one of the most reliable people for a job like his—if it weren't for one strange thing. Twice while we talked, he stopped, went pale, and looked toward the little bell even though it hadn't rung. He opened the door (which was usually kept shut to block the damp air) and stared out at the red signal light near the tunnel. Both times, he came back to the fire with that same strange expression I'd seen earlier, the one I couldn't quite describe.

As I stood to leave, I said, "You've almost convinced me you're a truly content man."

(I have to admit—I only said that to encourage him to talk more.)

"I think I used to feel that way," he said softly, just like when he first spoke. "But now… something's not right. I've been feeling really uneasy."

He seemed to wish he hadn't said it, but it was too late. Since he'd already brought it up, I asked quickly,

"What's bothering you? What's going on?"

"It's really hard to explain," he said. "Very hard to say out loud. But if you visit me again, I'll try to tell you then."

"I will," I promised. "When should I come back?"

"I leave early in the morning, but I'll be back on shift by ten tomorrow night."

"I'll come at eleven," I told him.

He nodded and walked with me to the door. "I'll shine my white light," he said in a low voice, "until you've found the path. But once you do, don't call out. And when you get to the top, stay quiet."

The way he said it gave me a chill, but I only replied, "Alright."

He added, "And tomorrow night, when you come down the path— don't call out then either. But let me ask you one last question. Why did you shout, 'Hey! Below there!' earlier tonight?"

"I don't know," I said. "I said something like that—"

"No," he cut in. "Not something like it. Those were your exact words. I know them perfectly."

"Okay, yes, I did say those words. I must've said them because I saw you standing there."

"No other reason?"

"What other reason could there be?"

"You didn't feel like someone—or something—put those words in your head?"

"No. Definitely not."

He told me goodnight and raised his light. I walked beside the track, feeling nervous the whole way—like a train could appear behind me at any moment—until I found the path. Going up was easier than coming down, and I reached my inn without any problems.

The next night, right on schedule, I stepped onto the zigzag path as the distant town clocks struck eleven. He was already waiting below, holding his white light.

"I didn't call out," I said once we were face to face. "Can I speak now?"

"Of course, sir."

"Good evening, then. Here's my hand."

"Good evening, sir. And here's mine."

We walked side by side to his small shelter, went inside, shut the door behind us, and sat by the fire.

"I've made up my mind," he said, leaning toward me and speaking just above a whisper. "I'm not going to make you ask twice what's been bothering me. Last night, I thought you were someone else. That's what's been weighing on me."

"You mean because you mistook me for someone?" I asked.

"No. I mean the person I mistook you for."

"Who is it?"

"I don't know."

"Do they look like me?"

"I'm not sure. I've never seen their face. They always cover it with their left arm. The right arm waves—wildly, like this."

He demonstrated the motion. It looked like someone waving in a panic, desperately trying to warn others—as if to say, "For God's sake, get out of the way!"

"One night, under the bright moonlight," the man said, "I was sitting here when I suddenly heard someone shout, 'Hey! Down there!' I jumped up, looked out that door, and saw someone standing by the red signal light near the tunnel, waving just like I showed you earlier. The voice sounded hoarse and loud, like they'd been yelling for a long time. It kept shouting, 'Look out! Look out!' and again, 'Hey! Down there! Look out!' I grabbed my lamp, turned the light red, and ran toward the person, calling out, 'What's wrong? What happened? Where is it?' The figure was just outside the tunnel. I got so close that I wondered why they were still covering their eyes with their sleeve. I reached out to pull the sleeve away—but the figure vanished."

"Did it go into the tunnel?" I asked.

"No. I ran in about five hundred yards. I stopped, raised my lamp, saw the distance markers, and noticed wet streaks running down the tunnel walls and dripping from the arch. I ran out faster than I had gone in. I was filled with dread. I checked around the red light with my lamp, climbed the metal ladder to the platform above it, climbed down again, and rushed back here. I sent a message both ways: 'An alarm has been given. Is there anything wrong?' The answer came back from both directions: 'Everything is fine.'"

A chill crawled down my spine, but I tried to shake it off. I told him the figure might've just been something his eyes made up—maybe a result of stress or nerve issues. It's not unusual. People sometimes see things like that when they're unwell. Some have even proven it through tests on themselves. "And about the voice," I said, "just listen to how the wind whistles through this weird valley. The telegraph wires sound like a sad, ghostly instrument."

He listened quietly for a while, then said he knew the sounds of the wind and wires better than anyone—he'd spent many long winter nights here alone. But he added that he wasn't done telling his story.

I apologized, and he gently touched my arm as he continued.

"Six hours after I saw that figure, there was a terrible crash on this railway line. And ten hours later, they brought the injured and the dead through the tunnel—right over the same spot where I had seen the figure standing."

A cold feeling swept over me, but I did my best to hide it. I told him that was a really strange coincidence, one that could leave a deep impression. But I also said that coincidences happen all the time, and we have to keep that in mind. Still, I admitted—before he could argue—that most logical people don't rely too much on coincidences when they make serious decisions.

He told me again he wasn't finished.

I apologized for interrupting.

"This," he said, placing his hand on my arm again and glancing over his shoulder with a fearful look, "was exactly one year ago. About six or seven months passed, and I had mostly gotten over it. But one morning, just as the sun was rising, I stood at the door, looked toward the red light—and saw the ghost again." He paused and stared at me.

"Did it yell anything?"

"No. It didn't make a sound."

"Did it wave at you?"

"No. It leaned on the signal post with its face covered by both hands. Like this."

I watched as he showed me. It looked like someone in mourning. I'd seen statues in cemeteries in the same pose.

"Did you go up to it?"

"I went inside and sat down. I needed time to think, and I felt lightheaded. When I opened the door again, it was already daylight—and the ghost was gone."

"But nothing happened afterward? No incident?"

He tapped my arm a few times with his finger and nodded, giving me a dark, unsettling look.

"That same day, as a train came out of the tunnel, I saw a blur at one of the windows—hands and heads, something waving. I managed to signal the driver just in time. He slowed down and used the brakes, but the train didn't stop until it had passed by about 150 yards. I chased after it, and while I ran, I heard screams and crying. A young woman had died instantly in one of the train cars. They brought her here and laid her right between us on this floor."

Without thinking, I pushed my chair back and stared at the part of the floor he pointed to.

"It's all true, sir. Exactly how it happened. That's what I'm telling you."

I couldn't think of anything helpful to say. My mouth was dry. Outside, the wind and wires seemed to carry the weight of the story with a long, sorrowful sound.

He went on. "Now, sir, try to understand why I'm so shaken. The ghost came back a week ago. Since then, it's been showing up off and on."

"At the warning signal?" I asked.

"Yes. At the Danger-light."

"What does it do?"

He repeated, even more emotionally than before, the motion of waving and shouting, "For God's sake, clear the way!"

Then he continued, "I can't sleep or relax because of it. It calls out to me, over and over, in a voice full of pain—'Down there! Look out! Look out!' It waves at me. It rings my little bell—"

I jumped in. "Are you saying it rang your bell last night while I was here, and you went to the door?"

"Twice."

"But that's impossible," I said. "I was watching the bell. I was listening closely, and I promise it didn't ring. Not then, not any other time—except when the station signaled."

He shook his head. "I've never mixed them up, sir. I can always tell the ghost's ring from the regular one. The ghost's bell gives off a weird, unnatural vibration. It doesn't feel anything like a real signal. And I never said the bell moves in a way you can see. It makes sense that you didn't hear it. But I definitely did."

"Did it look like the ghost was really there when you looked?"

"It was there."

"Both times?"

He replied with certainty, "Both times."

"Would you come with me to the door now and check if it's back?"

He bit his lower lip like he didn't really want to, but stood up. I opened the door and stepped outside while he stayed in the doorway. We could see the Danger-light, the dark tunnel entrance, the tall, damp stone walls on both sides, and the stars above us.

"Do you see it?" I asked, watching his face closely. His eyes were wide and tense, though probably no more than mine had been earlier when I stared at the same place.

"No," he said. "It's not there."

"Alright," I said.

We went back inside, closed the door, and sat down again. I was thinking of how I might take advantage of this moment—if it even counted as one—when he started talking again, as if it was obvious that everything he'd seen was real. He spoke with such certainty that I suddenly felt unsure of everything.

"You understand now," he said, "what really troubles me is this question—what does the ghost mean?"

I told him I wasn't sure I fully understood.

"What is it warning me about?" he asked, staring into the fire, only glancing at me every now and then. "What's the danger? Where is it? I feel like something awful is going to happen somewhere along the tracks. After what's already happened, I can't doubt that this third time is a real warning. But it's so cruel—why is it haunting me? What am I supposed to do?"

He took out a handkerchief and wiped the sweat from his forehead.

"If I send a warning signal to either side—or both—I won't be able to explain why," he continued, wiping his hands nervously. "I'd get in trouble, and it wouldn't help anyone. People would think I was crazy. It would go something like this: I send a message saying, 'Danger! Be careful!' They reply, 'What danger? Where?' I say, 'I don't know. But please, be careful!' And they'd fire me. What else could they do?"

The worry on his face was heartbreaking. He looked like someone carrying a heavy burden he didn't understand, but one that could cost lives if ignored.

"When it first appeared under the Danger-light," he said, running his fingers through his hair and rubbing his temples like he was overwhelmed, "why didn't it tell me where the accident was going to happen—if it had to happen? Why didn't it tell me how to stop it—if it could be stopped? Then, the second time, when it covered its face—why didn't it say, 'She's going to die. Keep her at home'? If it showed up both times just to prove its warnings were real and to prepare me for the third, then why not just be clear with me now? Why not give a direct warning? And why come to me of all people? I'm just a poor signalman at a lonely post. Why not go to someone important—someone people would believe and who could actually do something?"

When I saw how upset he was, I knew the best thing I could do—for his sake and for everyone's safety—was to help him calm down. I didn't argue about whether the ghost was real. Instead, I told him that what really mattered was doing his job the right way. Even if he didn't understand the strange things happening, he could still be proud that he was doing his duty. This helped more than trying to talk him out of what he believed. He began to settle down, and as the night went on, his work kept him focused. I left around two in the morning. I had offered to stay, but he said no.

I won't pretend I didn't look back at the red light more than once as I walked up the path. I didn't like it then, and I wouldn't have slept well if I'd had to sleep near it. I also didn't feel at ease about the two strange events—the crash and the girl's death—that had followed the ghost's visits. I can't pretend those didn't bother me.

But what I couldn't stop thinking about was: What should I do with what he told me? I knew this man was smart, alert, and careful—but how long would he stay that way under so much pressure? Even though he had a lower-ranking job, it was still a huge responsibility. Would I, for example, feel safe depending on him with my own life?

I couldn't shake the feeling that it would be wrong to report him to his superiors without speaking to him first. So I made up my mind to suggest a middle ground: I would offer to go with him to the best doctor we could find nearby. He had told me that his shift would change the next night—he'd be off duty an hour or two after sunrise and back again by sunset. I said I'd return then.

The next evening was beautiful, and I left early to enjoy a walk. The sun hadn't set yet when I passed the field path near the top of the deep cutting. I decided to walk for about an hour—half an hour out and half an hour back—then go straight to the signalman's post.

Before continuing, I stepped to the edge and looked down from the same spot where I had first seen him. A sudden chill ran through me when I saw what looked like a man near the tunnel entrance, covering his face with one arm and waving wildly with the other.

The feeling of dread quickly faded, though, because I realized it really was a man—and he wasn't alone. A small group stood nearby, and it looked like he was showing them how to do something. The Danger-light hadn't been turned on yet. Near it was a small shelter I hadn't seen before, made of wood and covered in tarpaulin. It was about the size of a bed.

A terrible sense of something being wrong hit me. I was filled with guilt, suddenly afraid that something bad had happened because I had left him alone without getting help. I rushed down the steep path as fast as I could.

"What happened?" I asked the group of men.

"The signalman died this morning, sir."

"You mean the one who worked in that box?"

"Yes, sir."

"You mean the man I spoke with?"

"If you knew him, sir, you'll recognize him," one of the men said softly. He removed his hat and gently lifted a corner of the tarp. "His face looks peaceful."

"Oh no... how did it happen?" I asked, turning from one man to the next as they covered him again.

"He was hit by a train, sir. No one knew the job better than he did. But somehow, he didn't step clear of the rail. It was just after sunrise. He had already turned on the light and was holding the lamp in his hand. When the train came out of the tunnel, he had his back to it, and it struck him. That man over there was the driver. He was showing us what happened. Go ahead, Tom."

The driver, dressed in a rough, dark outfit, stepped back toward the mouth of the tunnel.

"When we came around the curve," he said, "I saw him at the end of the track. It looked like I was seeing him through a long lens. There was no time to slow down. I knew he was always careful. But when he didn't react to the whistle, I turned it off and shouted as loud as I could."

"What did you shout?"

"I said, 'Below there! Look out! Look out! For God's sake, clear the way!'"

I froze.

"It was horrible, sir. I kept shouting. I covered my eyes with one arm so I wouldn't see the moment it happened, and I waved the other arm until the very end. But it didn't make a difference."

I won't drag out the story by focusing too much on any one strange detail. But I do have to point out something that shook me: the train driver's warning included not only the exact words the signalman had told me the ghost repeated, but also the exact same arm movements I had imagined—though I'd never said them out loud.

The End

Thank You for Reading

Dear Reader,

We hope this timeless classic has sparked your imagination and enriched your literary journey. Now that you've turned the final page, we want to share a vision for the future of reading—one where every classic you've ever wanted to explore is at your fingertips, in a format that best suits your life.

We'd like to invite you to gain immediate, unlimited digital & audiobook access to hundreds of the most treasured literary classics ever written—along with the option to secure deluxe paperback, hardcover & box set editions at printing cost. Together, we can spark a new global literary renaissance alongside our small, independent publishing house called "The Library of Alexandria."

Thousands of years ago, the Library of Alexandria stood as a beacon of knowledge—until it was lost to history. We aim to reignite that spirit of preservation and discovery right now, in the modern age—only this time, it's accessible to all, in every language and every format.

Picture a world where every timeless classic, novel, poem, or philosophical treatise is not only available to read but also updated for today's readers—modernized, translated into any language or dialect, and ready to enjoy in any format you choose, whether that is in an eBook, audiobook, paperback, or deluxe hardcover & box set version a printing cost.

By joining our movement to rebuild the modern Library of Alexandria, you become part of an unprecedented mission to offer:

- **Unlimited Audiobook & eBook Access to the Greatest Classics of All Time**

  Instantly explore thousands of legendary works, from Plato and Shakespeare to Jane Austen and Leo Tolstoy. All are instantly ready to read or listen to, giving you a complete literary universe at your fingertips.

- **Paperback & Deluxe Editions at Printing Costs:**

  Purchase any title in a paperback, deluxe hardbound, or deluxe boxset edition at printing costs, shipped right to your doorstep. Curate your personal library of Alexandria with editions worthy of display—crafted to last, designed to captivate, and delivered straight to your door.

- **Modern translations for Contemporary Readers in all languages and dialects**

  Discover a vast selection of classics reimagined in clear, current language—no more struggling with outdated phrases or obscure references. Next to the original versions, we aim to offer translations in as many languages and dialects as possible.

  As we continue our translation efforts and add new languages, readers everywhere can connect with these works as if they were written today. By bridging linguistic divides, you're contributing to ensuring that these timeless stories become more meaningful, accessible, and inspiring for people across the globe.

- **Your Personal Library of Alexandria:**

  Over the months and years, you'll curate a unique physical archive of classics—each volume a testament to your taste, curiosity, and love of knowledge. It's not just about owning books—it's about curating a cultural legacy you'll cherish and pass down for generations to come.

- **Join a Global Literary Renaissance:**

  Your support fuels an ongoing mission: allowing us to reinvest in offering deluxe print editions (including special boxsets) at their true cost, broaden the range of available formats and translations, and extend the reach of these works to new audiences worldwide. By joining today, you're not just preserving a legacy of masterpieces; you set in motion a powerful wave of literary accessibility.

  We are more than a publisher—we're a movement, and we can't do it alone. Your support lets us scale our mission, preserving and reimagining history's greatest works for tomorrow's readers.

Become a Torchbearer of knowledge.

Thank you for picking up this book and allowing us into your literary journey. As you turn the pages, know that you're part of something larger: a global effort to keep these stories alive, share their wisdom across borders and generations, and spark a true cultural revival for the modern era.

If this resonates with you—please consider taking the next step by visiting:

www.libraryofalexandria.com

With gratitude and a shared love of knowledge,

The Modern Library of Alexandria Team

Visit:

www.libraryofalexandria.com

Or scan the code below: